THE FUNNIEST DINOSAUR JOKE BOOK EVER

By Joe King

Illustrated by Nigel Baines

ANDERSEN PRESS

First published in 2018 by
Andersen Press Limited
20 Vauxhall Bridge Road
London SW1V 2SA
www.andersenpress.co.uk

2 4 6 8 10 9 7 5 3

British Library Cataloguing in Publication Data
available.

ISBN 978 1 78344 648 3

Printed and bound in Great Britain by Clays Limited,
Bungay, Suffolk, NR35 1ED

Dynamite Dinos

**What do you call a
sleeping dinosaur?**
A dino-snore

What do you call a dinosaur with no eyes?

Doyouthinkhesawus

What do you call a dinosaur with no eyes' dog?

Doyouthinkhesawus Rex

What does a Triceratops sit on?

Its Tricera-bottom

How do you raise a baby dinosaur?

With a crane

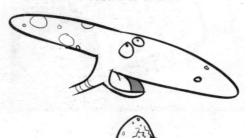

What do you call a dinosaur who's always on time?

Prontosaurus

What do you call a dinosaur with a good vocabulary?

Thesaurus

What does a dinosaur say when he shoots a goal in football?

'Dino-score!'

What do you call a popstar in the Jurassic age?

Miley Saurus

4

What does one Apatosaurus say to the other when they bump into each other?

'Small world, isn't it?'

What game does the Brontosaurus like to play with humans?

Squash

How do you know if there is a dinosaur in your refrigerator?

The door won't shut

How else do you know if there's a dinosaur in your refrigerator?

There are footprints in the butter

What did the dinosaur call her T-shirt-making business?

Try Sara's Tops

What do dinosaurs use on the floors of their kitchens?

Rep-tiles

Why was the Stegosaurus such a good volleyball player?

Because he could really spike the ball

What side of a dinosaur has the most scales?

The outside

What goes down but not up?

A Giganotosaurus in an elevator

**Who leaves presents
under a Velociraptor's
Christmas tree?**

Santa Claws

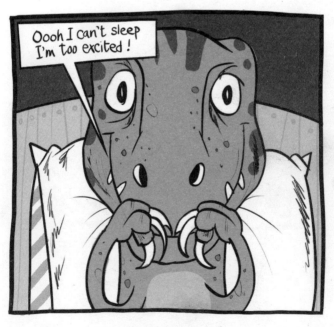

Why did the dinosaur cross the road?

It was the chicken's day off

Why didn't the dinosaur cross the road?

There weren't any roads then

Boy: Why did the Spinosaurus
cross the road?
*Girl: He didn't, the chicken
crossed the road.*
Boy: Well, why did the chicken
cross the road?
*Girl: To get away from the
Spinosaurus!*

**What did the dinosaur use to
build his house?**

A dino-saw

**Where did Noah put
the dinosaurs?**

On the Jurassic ark

Why do dinosaurs climb trees?

There's nothing else to climb in the jungle

What dinosaur would Harry Potter be?

A dino-sorcerer

What came after the dinosaur?

Its tail

How do you keep a dinosaur from smelling?

Cut off his nose

Why did the dinosaur get in the bed?

Because he was tired

What did the dinosaur say after the car crash?

'I'm so saur!'

Why don't dinosaurs ever forget?

Because no one ever tells them anything

What do you call a dinosaur that won't take a bath?

Extinks

What do you call a plated dinosaur when he is asleep?

Stegosnorus

Receptionist: Doctor, there's
an invisible dinosaur in
the waiting room.
Doctor: Tell her I can't see her!

**What do you call a
prehistoric hip-hop star?**

A raptor

**What do you say when you
meet a two-headed dinosaur?**

'Hello, hello!'

Boy: I lost my pet dinosaur.
*Girl: Why don't you put an
ad in the newspaper?*
Boy: What good would that do,
she can't read!

**What kind of dinosaur can
you ride in a rodeo?**

A Broncosaurus

**What makes more noise
than a dinosaur?**

Two dinosaurs

**What's the difference between
dinosaurs and dragons?**

*Dinosaurs are still too
young to smoke*

**How can you tell there's an
Allosaurus in your bed?**

*By the bright red 'A' on
its pyjamas*

14

Girl: Hey, what's wrong
with your foot?
*Boy: Well, did you see that
Diplodocus over there?*
Girl: Yes.
Boy: Well, I didn't!

What do you get if you feed a Spinosaurus lots of lemons?

A dino-sour

What do you call a Stegosaurus with carrots in its ears?

*Anything you want,
it can't hear you*

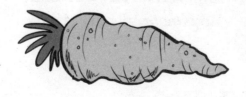

15

**What's better than a
talking dinosaur?**

A spelling bee

**What do you call a dinosaur
that never gives up?**

A Try-try-tryceratops

**What do you get when you
cross a dinosaur
with fireworks?**

Dino-mite

**How do you know if there's a
Diplodocus under your bed?**

Your nose hits the ceiling

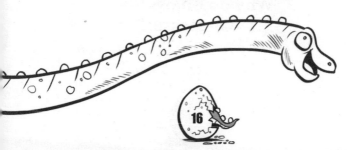

When can three giant dinosaurs get under an umbrella and not get wet?

When it's not raining

Why do dinosaurs wear glasses?

To make sure they don't step on other dinosaurs

What do you get when you run after a Velociraptor?

Exhausted

Why did the Diplodocus lay his head on the ground?

He was afraid of heights

Which dinosaurs were the best police officers?

The Triceracops

How should you address a posh dinosaur?

Dino-sir

Which type of dinosaur could jump higher than a house?

Any kind – a house can't jump

What weighs 3000 kilos and sticks to the roof of your mouth?

A peanut butter-and-Stegosaurus sandwich

What do you call a dinosaur that left its armour out in the rain?

A Stegosaurust

**What do you get when
a dinosaur walks through
the strawberry patch?**

Strawberry jam

**Why did the dinosaur paint
her claws red?**

*So she could hide in the
strawberry patch*

Mum: Why are you crying?
*Girl: Because I wanted to get a
dinosaur for my baby brother.*
Mum: That's no reason to cry.
*Girl: Yes it is! No one would
trade me for him!*

**Where did Brachiosaurus
buy things?**

At the dino-store

What do you get if you cross a pig with a dinosaur?

Jurassic Pork

Do you know how long dinosaurs should be fed?

Exactly the same as short dinosaurs

What do you need to know to teach a dinosaur tricks?

More than the dinosaur

How did the dinosaur feel after he ate a pillow?

Down in the mouth

What's worse than a giraffe with a sore throat?

A Diplodocus with a sore throat

Who makes the best prehistoric reptile clothes?

A dino-sewer

Why couldn't the dinosaur play games on the computer?

Because he ate the mouse

What did one dinosaur egg say to the other egg?

'Let's get crackin'!'

Which dinosaur had the cleanest teeth?

Flossoraptor

Did the dinosaur take a bath?

Why, is there one missing?

How many dinosaurs can fit in an empty box?

One. After that, the box isn't empty any more

Where do dinosaurs shop for games?

Toy-saur-us

What do you call a Stegosaurus with one leg?

Eileen

What do you get when a dinosaur sneezes?

Out of the way

Knock, knock
Who's there?
Dinosaur
Dinosaur who?
Dinosaurs don't go who, they go roar

What is an Iguanodon's favourite playground toy?

A dino-see-saw

What is in the middle of dinosaurs?

The letter 's'

What do you get if you cross a dog with a dinosaur?

Jurassic bark

What has a spiked tail, plates on its back, and sixteen wheels?

A Stegosaurus on roller-skates

What happened when the dinosaur took the train home?

She had to bring it back

What do you get if you cross a Triceratops with a kangaroo?

A Tricerahops

Why can't dinosaurs play the piano?

They're all dead

Why did the Diplodocus devour the factory?

Because she was a plant eater

What do you get if you cross a dinosaur with Mexican food?

A Tacosaurus

What did dinosaurs have that no other animals have?

Baby dinosaurs

Can you name ten dinosaurs in ten seconds?

Yes, one Ankylosaurus and nine Velociraptors

What is a dinosaur after he is five days old?

Six days old

T. Rex Titters

What did the Tyrannosaurus rex put on her steak?

Dino-sauce

**What kind of coat does
a T. rex wear?**

A Jurassic parka

**Is it true that a T. rex
won't hurt you if you hold
a tree branch?**

*That depends on how fast
you can run with it*

**Why do dinosaur parties
always go wrong?**

Because T. rex everything

**What did the
Tyrannosaurus rex get
after mopping the floor?**

Dino-sore arms

What is a T. rex's favourite number?

Ate

What is the best thing to do if you see a Tyrannosaurus rex?

Pray that he doesn't see you

**What do you call someone
who put their right hand in
the mouth of a T. rex?**

Lefty

**What vehicle does a T. rex use
to go from planet to planet?**

A dino-saucer

What do you get when dinosaurs crash their cars?

Tyrannosaurus wrecks

How do dinosaurs pay their bills?

With Tyrannosaurus cheques

Why do tyrannosaurs eat raw meat?

Because they don't know how to cook

What do you call a tyrannosaur that talks and talks and talks?

A dino-bore

**What do you call a T. rex
in a phone box?**

Stuck

**What should you do if you
find a T. rex in your bed?**

Find somewhere else to sleep

What's the best way to talk to a tyrannosaur?

Long distance

What do you get when you cross a T. rex and a snowman?

Frostbite

What is T. rex's most hated exercise?

Push-ups

What is T. rex's favourite food?

Baked beings

What's a dinosaur's favourite drink?

Tea rex

What does a T. rex call a Velociraptor?

Fast food

What do you call a short-sighted dinosaur?

Tyrannosaurus specs

**What do you call
Tyrannosaurus rex
when it wears a cowboy
hat and boots?**

Tyrannosaurus Tex

**What made the dinosaur's
car stop?**

A flat Tyreannosaurus

**Why didn't the T. rex take
ballet lessons?**

She outgrew her leotard

How does a T. rex smell?

Awful

Why did the Tyrannosaurus rex stand on one leg?

Because it would fall over if it lifted the other one

Why did the T. rex cross the road?

To eat the chicken on the other side

Terrible Pterosaurs

What do you get if you cross a duck with a flying dinosaur?

A pteroquacktyl

What was the scariest prehistoric animal?

The terrordactyl

What did pterodactyl say when it was flying?

'I can saur!'

What do you get if you cross an ox with a flying dinosaur?

A pteroyaktyl

Girl: I keep seeing Pteranodons with orange polka dots.
Boy: Have you seen an eye doctor yet?
Girl: No, just Pteranodons with orange polka dots!

Why did the Archaeopteryx catch the worm?

Because it was an early bird

Why did the Archaeopteryx cross the road?

Because chickens weren't invented yet

What do you get when you cross an Archaeopteryx with a lawnmower?

Shredded tweet

Why can't you hear a pterodactyl going to the toilet?

Cos the 'p' is silent

What time is it when a pterosaur lands on your bed?

Time to get a new bed

Why did the pterodactyl get a fine?

It broke the law of gravity

What's as big as a Quetzalcoatlus but weighs nothing?

Its shadow

What was twelve metres long, had a huge beak, and left crumbs all over the mattress?

The Pretzelcoatlus

What do you get if you cross a dinosaur with a flying horse?

A Pegasaurus

Why did the flying dinosaur miss the party?

It was feeling under the feather

Where was the pterodactyl flying when the sun went down?

In the dark

What is a Pteranodon when it's no longer there?

Pterano-gone

Why did the dinosaur evolve wings?

It wanted a bird's-eye view

Sea
Monster
Sillies

How many eyes does an
ichthyosaur have?

One 'i' at the front

How do you know if a plesiosaur is in your swimming pool?

There are great big puddles everywhere

Why was the plesiosaur afraid of the ocean?

Because there was something fishy about it

Why did the plesiosaur blush?

Because the sea weed

Where do prehistoric swimming reptiles like to go on holiday?

To the dino-shore

What do you call a plesiosaur with no fins floating in the sea?

Bob

How does a plesiosaur greet a fish?

'Pleased to eat you!'

What do you do if you find a blue ichthyosaur?

Cheer him up

What do you call a polite swimming dinosaur?

A pleaseyosaur

Why don't ichthyosaurs pass their exams?

Because they work below C level

Why do you never ask a plesiosaur to read you a story?

Because their tales are so long

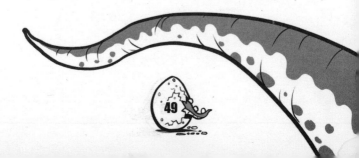

How do you make a plesiosaur float?

Put a scoop of ice cream in a glass of Coca-Cola and add one plesiosaur

Where do plesiosaurs sleep?

On the sea bed

What does a giant plesiosaur eat?

Anything she wants

Why did the ichthyosaur swim in the sea?

Because there were no swimming pools around then

Why did the ichthyosaur cross the sea?

To get to the other tide

Why is a plesiosaur easy to weigh?

Because it has its own scales

What do you call the mushy stuff between a plesiosaur's teeth?

Slow swimmers

Paleo Puns

What do you call a fossil that doesn't ever want to work?

Lazy bones

What did the dinosaur say to the woolly mammoth?

'I existed before it was cool.'

What did the dinosaur say to the asteroid?

'Comet me, dude!'

Why do mammoths have trunks?

Because they'd look silly carrying suitcases

Why are there old dinosaur bones in the museum?

Because they can't afford new ones

What did one paleontologist say to the other paleontologist?

'I've got a bone to pick with you.'

Girl: I wish I had enough money to buy a dinosaur skeleton.
Boy: *What would you do with a dinosaur skeleton?*
Girl: Who wants a skeleton? I just want the money!

Why was the dinosaur silent?

Because it was petrified

What did the asteroid say before it killed the dinosaurs?

'I'm going to rock your world!'

How do dinosaurs pass exams?

With extinction

What do woolly mammoths wear when they go swimming?

Their trunks

What did the dinosaur say when he saw the volcano erupt?

'What a lavaly day!'

Why didn't the T. rex skeleton attack the museum visitors?

Because she had no guts

Why shouldn't you make fun of a paleontologist?

Because you will get Jurasskicked

How much memory does a prehistoric computer have?

One trilobyte

What fossil only comes out in the dark?

Ammonight

Why did the supercontinent split up?

Because there was too much friction going on

Why did Pangaea break up?

It was faulty

What kind of music do geologists like?

Rock songs

What do you call a woolly mammoth in the desert?

Lost

Why do paleontologists like fossils so much?

Because they dig them

Which is a dinosaur's least favourite reindeer?

Comet

What did the dinosaur say when the volcano exploded?

'Don't erupt while I'm talking.'

What did the other dinosaur say when the volcano erupted?

'This is a catashtrophe!'

What did the paleontologist say when she discovered a coprolite?

'Oh, poo!'